This book should be returned to any Lancashire
County Council Library on or before the date shown

Lancashire County Library,
County Hall Complex,
2nd floor Christ Church Precinct,
Preston, PR1 8XJ

www.lancashire.gov.uk/libraries

Lancashire
County
Council

LL1(A)

For Our Ted

First published 2021 by Walker Books Ltd

87 Vauxhall Walk, London SE11 5HJ

2 4 6 8 10 9 7 5 3 1

© 2020 Brun Limited

The right of Anthony Browne to be identified as the author and illustrator of this work has been

asserted by him in accordance with the Copyright, Designs and Patents Act 1988

This book has been typeset in Bembo Educational

Printed in China

British Library Cataloguing in Publication Data: a catalogue record for

this book is available from the British Library

ISBN 978-1-4063-9509-9

www.walker.co.uk

WALKER BOOKS

AND SUBSIDIARIES

LONDON • BOSTON • SYDNEY • AUCKLAND

ERNEST
THE ELEPHANT

ANTHONY BROWNE

Ernest lived with his mum and the rest of the herd.

Every day they walked and ate and drank. At night they slept.

Ernest was happy, walking and eating and drinking and sleeping,
but just lately he'd started to wonder what else there was in life.

One day they wandered past a jungle.

"What's that?" Ernest asked his mum.

"It's only a jungle," said Mum, "not a place for little baby elephants!"

But it looks wonderful, thought Ernest. *And anyway,*

I'm not a little baby elephant.

While his mum and the rest of the herd walked on, eating and drinking – and talking of course (I forgot to say that they talked, a lot) – Ernest slipped silently into the jungle. "Now for a bit of fun," he said quietly.

The jungle was like nothing he'd ever seen before – full of colour, dazzling light and mysterious dark shadows. Ernest was fascinated. *So this is the jungle. Exciting … but, just a little bit frightening.*

Ernest walked deeper and deeper into the jungle. After a while he stopped. *Perhaps I should go back now?* he thought. But which way had he come? He couldn't see a path anywhere and there was no one to ask, so he stumbled on through the undergrowth.

Eventually he came across a gorilla, chewing on a stick of bamboo. *Oh, thank goodness*, Ernest thought, *it looks like he knows his way around.*

"Excuse me," said Ernest, "can you help me? I'm lost and I need to find my way back to my mum."

"No," said the gorilla, "go away. Can't you see I'm busy?" He shoved the bamboo back into his mouth and carried on chewing noisily.

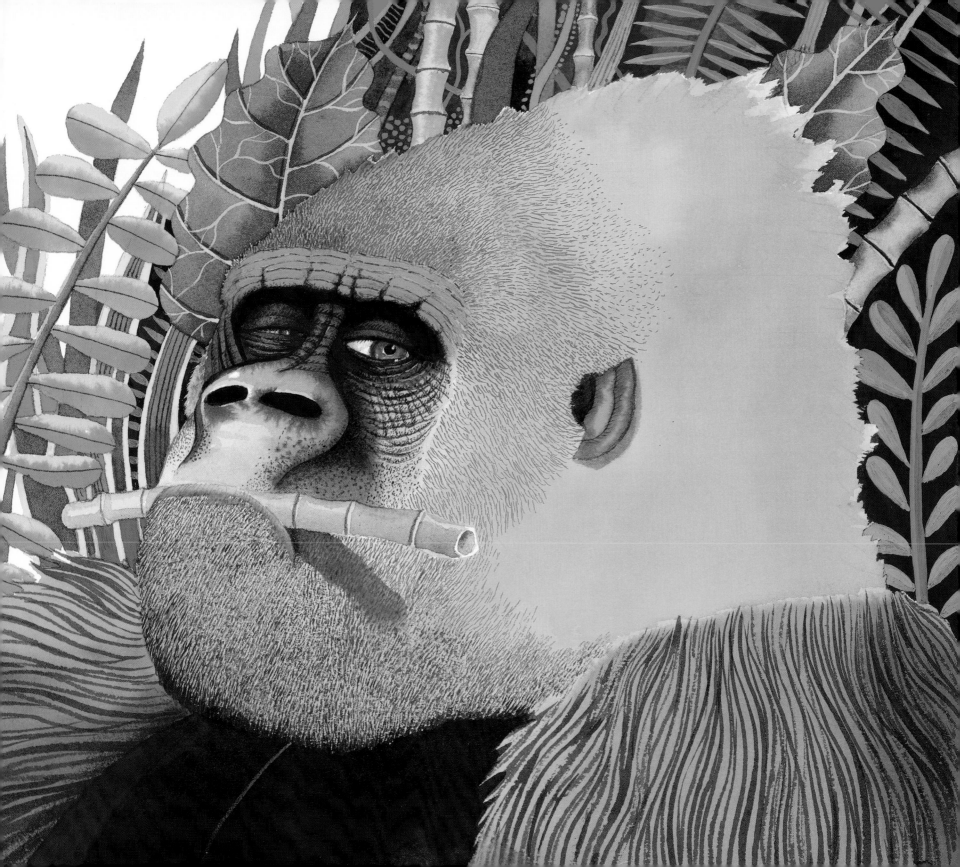

Oh well, thought Ernest and walked on into a clearing.
Soon he saw a lion, lying down in the grass.
"Excuse me," said Ernest, "can you help me?
I'm lost and I can't find my mum."

The lion opened one eye and looked at him for
a long, long time. Then he opened the other and said,
"No, why should I? Leave me alone,"
and closed his eyes.

Further on Ernest met a hippo, floating in the river.
"Excuse me," said Ernest, "can you help me? I'm lost
and I've got to find my mummy."

The hippo didn't even look at him.
"No," he yawned, "I'm not going to help you,"
and he floated away.

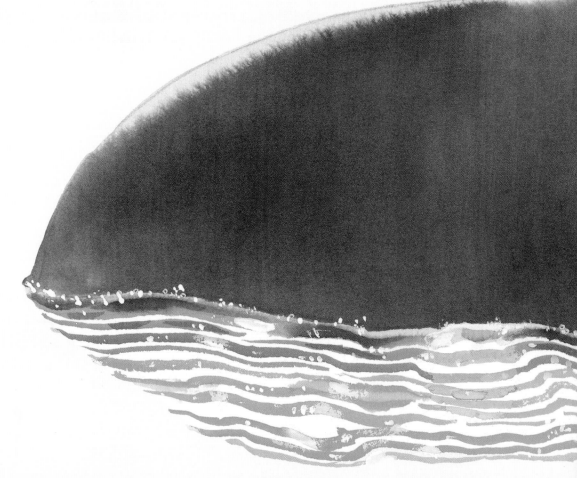

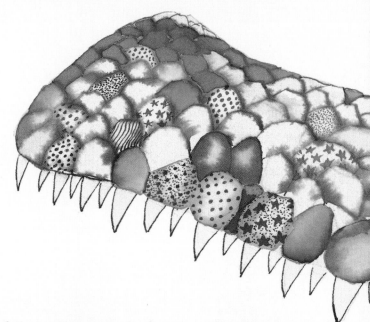

Ernest was getting really worried now. He felt as though he had a huge
lump in his throat. He saw a crocodile about to get into the water.
"Excuse me, can you help me – PLEASE? I've lost my mummy
and nobody cares."

The crocodile took one look at Ernest, slowly shook
his head, then disappeared underwater.

Ernest started to cry. How was he going to find his way back to
his mum when no one would help him? Suddenly he heard
a very quiet noise down by his feet.

"Don't be sad. Can I help you?" a little voice said.

Ernest looked down and there was a mouse.

"No, you won't be able to
help me," said Ernest. "I've
lost my mummy and now I
can't find my way out of the
jungle and I'll never ever
see her again."

"But I *can* help you," said the
mouse. "Lift me up and I'll
show you the way."

Ernest didn't really believe the mouse but he was so polite
that he carefully lifted him onto his head. It was better
to be lost with someone than lost all alone.

But the little mouse did know the way
and showed Ernest the path out of the jungle.
"ERNEST!" called Mum.

"MUM!" called Ernest.

"Oh my love," cried Mummy, "I'm so pleased to see you!
   I've been so worried."
"So have I," said Ernest.
   They were very, very happy,
   back together again.

(And so was the little mouse, as it
quietly scurried back into the jungle.)